Bridgette
Bitzan

Mr. Beetle

Mr. Beetle

SATOSHI
TADA

Translated by
Cathy Hirano

Carolrhoda Books, Inc. /Minneapolis

Yoshi loves bugs. **BEETLES** are his favorite kind.

One winter day, Yoshi found some rhinoceros beetle grubs in a forest far from home. One grub was HUGE.

Yoshi had never seen a grub that big before, so he decided to take it home.

Yoshi put the grub
in his yard.

The grub grew bigger and BIGGER.

At the end of June,
the grub rested as a
hard shell GREW OVER HIM.

All through July, the grub rested in the shell.

He **slowly** changed into a rhinoceros **BEETLE.**

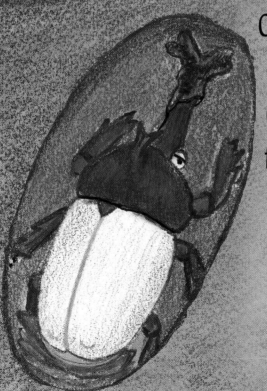

On a hot summer day, the beetle **crawled** from his shell.

And then...

The **ENORMOUS** beetle popped out of the ground.

Yoshi named his new friend "Mr. Beetle."

Hooray!

"Come on, Mr. Beetle,"
Yoshi said. "Let's go to
my room."

Yoshi sneaked into the kitchen to find a snack for Mr. Beetle.
"Here, Mr. Beetle," said Yoshi. "Let's have some watermelon."

Mr. Beetle
ate and ate
until he finished
the **WHOLE**
watermelon.

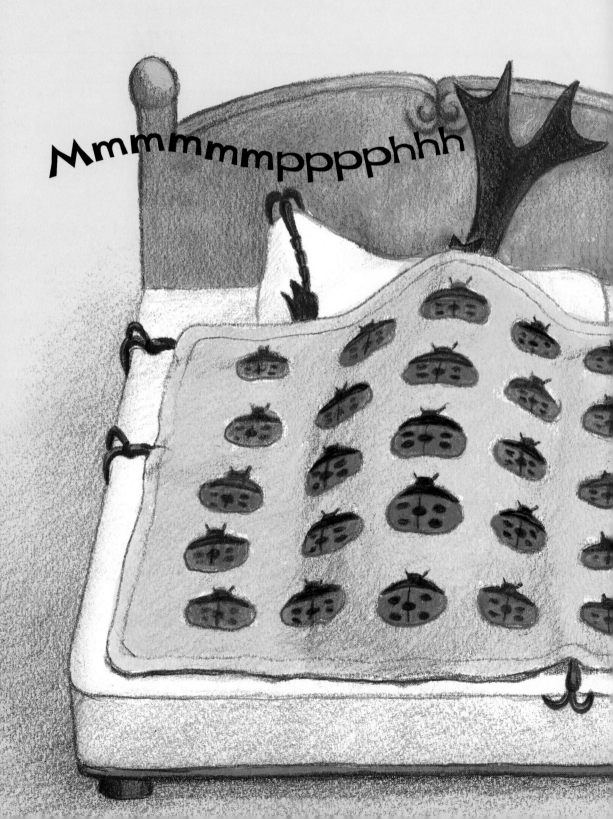

Wake up!

The next morning, Yoshi woke up early. He tried to tug Mr. Beetle out of bed. "Come on, Mr. Beetle! Wake up! Let's go outside and play." Finally Mr. Beetle muttered, "Okay, OKAY."

"Mr. Beetle sure is strong!"

Yoshi and his friends played with
Mr. Beetle at the park.

"Look how light he is!"

Mr. Beetle **WON** every game of jump rope.

"Play fair!" said Yoshi.

Mr. Beetle **banged** his horn at the bottom of the slide. "That's what you get for showing off!" Yoshi said.

CRASH!

Yoshi and Mr. Beetle **PLAYED** together all day. Then in the evening, they shared a bath. Mr. Beetle **bobbed UP** and **down** because he was so light.

"Yoshi! **HELP!**"

When they were clean, Yoshi helped
Mr. Beetle out of the tub.

"Who needs a towel
When you have
WINGS?"
Mr. Beetle thought.

That night, Yoshi fell **sound asleep.**
Mr. Beetle was wide awake. Night was
his favorite time, so he crawled out of bed.

He **sneaked** outdoors and **opened** his wings.

buzzed
Mr. Beetle's
wings.
He flew toward
bright, shining
lights.

MMMMMM

Mr. Beetle saw GLOWING city lights in the distance.

He ZOOMED over the city looking for something to eat. He didn't find anything. He thought the city was beautiful, but lonely. He missed Yoshi.

He flew swiftly back toward Yoshi's home.

When Yoshi woke up the next morning, Mr. Beetle was gone! Yoshi **RUSHED** outside and got on his bike. He raced down the street.

"Where are you, Mr. Beetle?"

Mr. Beetle **sniffed** the air with his antennae. He **found** Yoshi right away and landed.

"MR. BEETLE!"
Yoshi yelled happily.
"I'm **so glad** to
see you! How did you
find me?"

"I know your scent,"
Mr. Beetle said.

Even though he was with Yoshi, Mr. Beetle felt blue. "Mr. Beetle, don't you like fruit? Aren't you HUNGRY?" Yoshi asked.

"Yoshi, I want to live in a forest where I can drink tree sap," Mr. Beetle sighed. Yoshi remembered the forest where he had found Mr. Beetle.

In the evening, Yoshi climbed onto Mr. Beetle's back. **Mr. Beetle flew and flew and flew.** Yoshi pointed to a faraway forest. "There it is, Mr. Beetle! There's your home!" Yoshi called.

Mr. Beetle
shinnied up a
tree and tasted the
delicious sap.

When he saw how
HAPPY Mr. Beetle was,
Yoshi felt **GLAD** they
had come to the forest.

"Mr. Beetle, I wanted you to stay with me,"
he said, "But I can see that the forest is
YOUR HOME."
"Thank you for showing me how to get here,"
said Mr. Beetle.
"If I visit you, can we still
play together?"
asked Yoshi.
"You bet," said
Mr. Beetle.

It was late when Mr. Beetle gently lifted Yoshi, who had fallen asleep. He flew over the forest and town, carrying his FRIEND.

Mr. Beetle tucked Yoshi into bed.

"Goodnight,
Yoshi," said Mr. Beetle.
"Come visit me soon."

BEETLE FACTS

Mr. Beetle is a rhinoceros beetle. A
male rhinoceros beetle has a horn on his head and
a curved hook on his back. He uses his horn to
flip and shove other beetles in fights.
Female rhinoceros beetles have bumps instead
of horns.

Each of Mr. Beetle's six legs ends in a sharp claw, which
helps him climb. He closes his leathery back to protect his
wings. His back opens up to be a second set of wings.

Mr. Beetle's eyes have many lenses. Each lens lets him see
a different angle. Mr. Beetle's antennae stick out from his
head. Hairs and organs on the antennae can detect odors.
Mr. Beetle's mouth is surrounded by mouthparts that help
him eat. Some beetles eat other insects or other animals.
Mr. Beetle eats tree sap.
When he was a grub, he
ate rotting leaves
and wood.

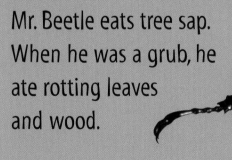

GROWING UP AS A BEETLE

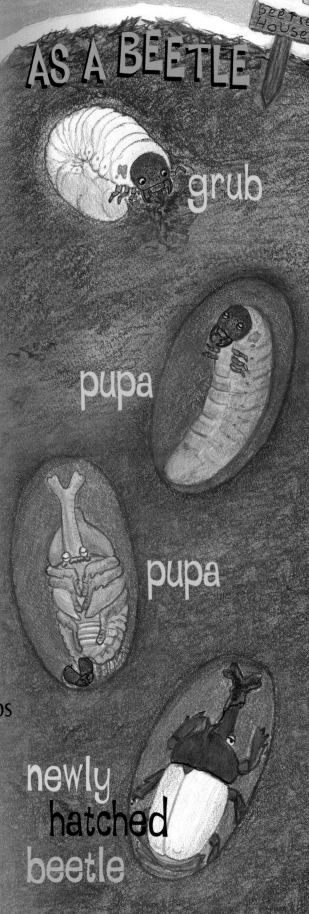

grub

pupa

pupa

newly hatched beetle

Female beetles lay tiny, soft eggs that hatch into grubs, or larva. As the grub grows, its skin stays the same size. When the skin is tight, the grub sheds it.

After it sheds three skins, the grub can't get any bigger. It's time to become a pupa. The grub makes a little hole, then a hard shell grows over the grub. This shell protects the grub while it changes into a beetle.

After a month as a pupa, the beetle hatches. The rhinoceros beetle's body is white. After about a day passes, the beetle's outer covering has hardened and darkened. The beetle is all grown up !

About the Author

Satoshi Tada was born in Tokyo in 1968. He has loved insects all his life. *Mr. Beetle* is his first picture book.

About the Translator

Cathy Hirano's translation of *The Friends* by Kazumi Yumoto (Farrar, Straus & Giroux) garnered the Mildred Batchelder Award. It also received the Boston Globe-Horn Book Award and the Hungry Mind Review Award, both for best fiction. Her work has made the IBBY Honor List for translation. Although Cathy grew up in Canada, she has lived in Japan since 1978.

First American edition published in 2001 by Carolrhoda Books, Inc.

First published in Japan in 1999 under the title *Kabuto-Kun* by Koguma Publishing Co., Ltd.
English translation rights arranged with Koguma Publishing, Co., Ltd.
through Japan Foreign-Rights Center.

The photo on page 46 is © Pam Gardner; Frank Lane Picture Agency/Corbis.

Designed by: Zachary Marell and Tim Parlin
Edited by: Katy Holmgren

Carolrhoda Books, Inc.
A division of Lerner Publishing Group
241 First Avenue North, Minneapolis, MN 55401

Website address: www.lernerbooks.com

Library of Congress Cataloging-in-Publication Data
Tada, Satoshi.
Mr. Beetle / written and illustrated by Satoshi Tada.
    p. cm.
Summary: A young boy befriends a giant beetle, taking it home to live with him, until they both see that the beetle needs to live in its real home, the forest.
    ISBN 1-57505-561-9 (lib. bdg.)
[1. Beetles—Fiction.] I. Title.
P27.T1163 Mr 2001
 [E] —dc21

                                    00-009697

Manufactured in the United States of America
1 2 3 4 5 6 - JR - 06 05 04 03 02 01

Bridgette
Bitzar